Annie Glover Is NOT a Tree Lover

Also by Darleen Bailey Beard

Operation Clean Sweep

The Babbs Switch Story

The Flimflam Man
(Pictures by Eileen Christelow)

Twister
(Pictures by Nancy Carpenter)

The Pumpkin Man from Piney Creek
(Pictures by Laura Kelly)

Annie
Glover
Is NOT a
Tree Lover

Darleen Bailey Beard
Pictures by Heather Maione

Farrar Straus Giroux
New York

Text copyright © 2009 by Darleen Bailey Beard
Pictures copyright © 2009 by Heather Maione
Distributed in Canada by Douglas & McIntyre Ltd.
Printed in August 2009 in the United States of America
by RR Donnelley, Harrisonburg, Virginia
Designed by Jay Colvin
First edition, 2009
1 3 5 7 9 10 8 6 4 2

www.fsgkidsbooks.com

Library of Congress Cataloging-in-Publication Data
Beard, Darleen Bailey.
    Annie Glover is not a tree lover / Darleen Bailey Beard ; pictures by
Heather Maione.— 1st ed.
        p.   cm.
    Summary: When her grandmother chains herself to the tree across
from the school to save it from being cut down, fourth-grader Annie
wants to die of humiliation, but when she discovers the town's history,
her attitude changes.
    ISBN: 978-0-374-30351-8
    [1. Trees—Fiction.   2. Protest movements—Fiction.
3. Environmental protection—Fiction.   4. Grandmothers—Fiction.]
I. Maione, Heather Harms, ill.   II. Title.

PZ7.B374 An 2009
[Fic]—dc22
                                                                2008043418

Dedicated to my parents, Larry and Ella Holman Bailey, for all their love and for taking my sister, Sherrie, and me on countless drives to show us the beauty of nature. To Aunt Janice and Uncle Claude Fite for all *their* love, too. And to two special teachers: Carmen Dorris, retired English teacher, who made front-page news and inspired this story; and Lorna Hodge, retired elementary teacher, whose friendship brightens my days. Finally, to a dear pal from high school, Lisa Robinett, who introduced me to FIS (Friends of International Students); and to my two students: Zhe Zhang in China and Jaroslav Hrdina in the Czech Republic.

CONTENTS

Annie
Glover
Is NOT a
Tree Lover

ELMER

no, Grandma. Don't make me do this."

"Come on now, Annie. Wrap this chain around me."

"No."

"Lock it."

"*Noooo.* I don't want to lock it. Besides, you can lock it without me."

Across the street, a bus groaned to a stop. Kids tumbled out, walking into Will Rogers Elementary. I turned my head and ducked down, hoping no one had seen me.

"Annie? Stop stallin' or you'll be late to school."

"Grand-ma."

"Just do it!"

Reluctantly, I wrapped the chain around Grandma.

"Now lock it," she said.

"Do you have the key?"

"Right here, Chickadee." She patted her coat pocket.

"Are you sure you—"

"Lock it!"

I clicked the padlock and Grandma was chained to a tree—an enormous American elm that had grown all crooked and bent—right across the street from my school.

"Now skedaddle," Grandma said, shooing me like a fly. "And don't worry about me and Elmer. We'll be just fine."

But I wasn't worried about Grandma or the stupid ol' tree she'd named Elmer. I was worried about *me* and what everyone at school would say.

So I quickly ran across the street, leaves crunching under my shoes.

Cornstalks and pumpkins greeted me as I stepped inside Will Rogers Elementary. A wheelbarrow stood by the office door with a sign that said: DONATE CANNED GOODS FOR THANKSGIVING BASKETS. Book-fair posters—CALLING ALL COWPOKES and ROPE A GOOD BOOK—covered the walls.

I bit my bottom lip, hoping no one would

notice Grandma through the big front windows and glass doors. But how could they *not*?

There she stood, on the other side of the street, in the large vacant lot that was the size of a football field. She had on her pink high-top tennis shoes, her puffy winter coat, and her plaid cap with earflaps. In one hand was a bullhorn. In the other, a sign that said SAVE OUR NATIVE TREE! Tied around the trunk was a "Happy Birthday" banner. And tucked into the banner was an Oklahoma flag and Bo-Bo Stinker Pot, my old brown teddy bear.

I glanced up and down the hall, then over my shoulder. *Good. No one has seen her yet.* So I hurried into Room 4B, hoping to blend in with all the other fourth-graders until someone noticed Grandma and my life was over.

"Annie-Ba-Nannie, isn't it fab? Like totally glorious? Bentley's getting a community swimming pool!"

"Yeah . . . glorious." I forced a smile at my best friend. Her real name was Elizabeth, but she went by Jazz because she said Elizabeth was as boring as cottage cheese.

She reached over and felt my forehead. "Are you sick? What's wrong?"

"Nothing."

"I know you better than that. Now out with it."

But how do you *out with it* when your very own grandmother's chained to a tree for the entire world to see and you feel like disappearing into a deep, dark hole?

"Just imagine," Jazz said. "Next summer . . . you and me . . . swimming every single day . . . getting *golden-licious* tans."

Jazz reminded me of a butterfly whose words were her wings. I never knew what word she'd take flight with next.

"Annie-Ba-Nannie, I don't get you today," Jazz said, wrinkling her eyebrows. "Here we are getting a cool pool right across the street. And you're not even happy? I'm telling you, girlfriend, there's something wrong here."

I hiked my shoulders then let them droop like overcooked noodles.

Kids buzzed into the room, hanging up their coats and stacking homework into Mrs. Hodge's homework basket. Their faces beamed and everyone talked at once.

"Did you hear about the pool?"

"Yeah, it's going to be ten feet deep. *Ten feet!*"

"With a high dive and a waterslide!"

"And a snack bar with Bahama Mama snow cones!"

"And a baby pool for Annie. Isn't that right, Annie-Fannie-Wannie?"

If anyone knew how to get under my skin, it was scrawny ol' Leroy Kirk. He was like a tick on a hound dog and no matter how hard I tried, I couldn't shake him off.

"Very funny," I said, shooting him a mean look.

Leroy was the type of kid who kept an emergency medical kit in his desk and carried his own travel-size box of Kleenex everywhere he went. Even at recess. And he smelled kind of funny—like a mixture of Mentholatum and the cotton from an aspirin bottle.

"The weatherman says we've got southerly breezes blowing up from Texas," he said. "That means my allergies are going to drive me nuts today. I'm allergic to grass, you know. And tree pollen drives me crazy. My throat gets all clogged and my eyes itch and my nose drips and—"

At last, the bell rang, saving me from Leroy and his daily allergy update. If he wasn't so annoying, I'd almost feel sorry for him.

"Good morning, class," Mrs. Hodge said.

Mrs. Hodge had the prettiest smile and red hair, just like Leroy's. But unlike Leroy's, hers was combed nice and soft, and didn't have a big flat spot in the back from where she'd slept the night before.

Leroy popped up from his seat and ran to the window. "Mrs. Hodge! Mrs. Hodge! Did you read the newspaper this morning? Did you hear the good news?"

"Leroy, sit back down," Mrs. Hodge said.

"But they're building a swimming pool right across the street! It's going to—" He stopped talking and pointed out the window. His mouth gaped open. "Look! There's an old man out there chained to that big tree!"

I gulped. Grandma *did* kind of look like an old man, especially from a distance. I kept quiet, crossing my fingers.

Everyone flocked to the window. Even Mrs. Hodge.

"Let me see. Oh my gosh!"

"What's he doing out there?"

"Can anyone read what his sign says?"

"Wait! That's not a man. That's a lady! See? She has pink shoes on!"

Drat those pink high-tops. I drooped down in my chair.

"Who is she?"

"Must be some kind of weirdo."

"Hey! I know who that is," Dixie Lurken said, snapping her fingers. "That's Annie's grandma! She lives with Annie down the street from me."

I drooped even droopier. *Thanks a lot, Miss Bigmouth.*

A FAKE BELLYACHE

et me guess! Let me guess!" Jazz said as we sat
down at lunch. "Your grandma's trying to raise
awareness for endangered wild zebras. Right?"

I took a sip of my milk. "Wrong. That was last
month."

The cafeteria was crowded and smelled of
spaghetti and strawberry Jell-O. I turned my lunch
sack upside down and shook it. Out flopped a
bologna and cheese sandwich, a bruised banana, a
bag of crunched-up potato chips, and an oatmeal
raisin cookie.

"I've got it," Jazz said. "She's protesting the
high price of gasoline."

"That was three months ago."

"Hmm . . . nuclear waste?"

"Last year."

"Pollution?"

I shook my head.

Jazz covered her heart. "Well, whatever it is, it's got to be really romantic."

"*Romantic?*" I stared at Jazz. "You think being chained to a tree is *romantic?*"

"Sure," Jazz said, taking flight with her words. "There she is . . . a lone woman . . . chained to a tree . . . a prisoner by choice. Don't you see? It's *deliciously* romantic."

I rolled my eyes. "Believe me. You wouldn't think it was deliciously romantic if it was *your* grandma out there."

"Yes I would," Jazz said. She opened her milk and scooted closer. "So tell me. It must be *totally* tragic."

Everything to Jazz was either deliciously romantic or totally tragic—or both. I once stepped on a spider—*a spider, for gosh sakes*—and she insisted we have a funeral for it.

"It's not tragic. And it's not romantic," I said. Then, looking over my shoulder to check for eavesdroppers, I cupped my hand over Jazz's ear and told her the whole dreaded story of how Grandma was trying to protect the tree from being cut down for the new swimming-pool complex. I even told her how Grandma had insisted on taking Bo-Bo Stinker Pot against my wishes as a last-minute mascot.

"Oh, Annie-Ba-Nannie! That *is* totally tragic. Why, it's the most totally tragic story I've ever heard." Then she grabbed both my hands. "Do you think they'll leave the tree and just move the pool over a little?"

"No," I said. "Grandma's talked to Mr. Castillo, Bentley's city manager, several times. He said they have to cut down the tree because it's taking up the place of ten parking spaces."

Jazz took a bite of spaghetti, then wiped the sauce off her chin. "I really, *really* want that swimming pool."

"Me, too."

"Can't they just have fewer parking spaces?"

"The city council said the tree has to go. They've already hired someone to cut it down this Monday. And what makes Grandma so mad is that the tree is over a hundred years old."

Jazz covered her heart again. "Over a hundred years old? Why, that's older than my great-great-aunt Ima, who only has one eye and lives in a nursing home."

I took a sip of my milk. "What happened to her eye?"

"I'm not exactly sure. My mom says it involves her one true love. Guess what his name was?"

"What?"

"Lawrence Pigg. That was his real name, too. Just think, if Great-Great-Aunt Ima had married him, her name would have been Ima Pigg. *Ima Pigg!* I'm telling you, it *had* to be true love with a name like that," Jazz said. "Anyway, they never married and Great-Great-Aunt Ima remained single and brokenhearted the rest of her entire life. When I get old enough, Mom says she's going to get out a big box of Kleenex and tell me the whole tragic story."

I poured some crunched-up potato chips into my mouth. Sometimes I wondered about that best friend of mine.

"You know," Jazz said, strawberry Jell-O wiggling on the end of her fork, "if I had the choice between a pool or a tree, I'd have to choose a pool. Wouldn't you?"

"Sure," I said. "A pool's a pool. Who wants a tree when you can have a pool?"

"But," Jazz said, "a hundred years is a hundred years. Just think of all the stories that tree could tell. Maybe even some totally tragic ones."

Leave it to Jazz to think about talking trees.

"So how long is she going to stay chained to that tree?"

"Till they put the pool somewhere else or until she's, you know"—I lowered my voice to an almost-silent whisper—"arrested."

"*Arrested?*" Jazz dropped her fork. "You mean she can get *arrested*?"

"Who's getting arrested?" Leroy asked, plopping down his lunch tray.

"Nobody," I said, hushing Jazz. "Nobody at all."

Leroy sat down and picked up my banana, pushing imaginary buttons as though he were dialing a cell phone. "Hello? Is this Annie's granny? This is the tree police. You're under arrest!"

I grabbed my banana, resisting the urge to smoosh it up his nose.

"Just admit it, Annie-Fannie-Wannie," Leroy said. "You know your grandma's crazy. Crazy as a lunatic."

"She is not!"

"Is too."

I gave him my meanest, coldest stare.

"Everybody in Bentley knows she's one nut away from the nut farm . . . has squirrels in her attic . . . is loopier than an airplane . . . fruitier than a fruitcake!"

I rolled my eyes. "Come on, Jazz. Let's get out of here."

We wolfed down our lunches, and then stepped outside. Zipping our coats, we walked around the playground and settled on the side steps of the cafeteria.

"Don't let Leroy get you down," Jazz said. "He's just a skinny little jerk who doesn't know what he's talking about."

True.

"He's so skinny, if he stood sideways, you'd think he was a straw!"

True again.

"If you ask me, Leroy's so skinny, he'd make good dental floss!"

I laughed, tilting my head back, letting the sun splash my face.

"Oh my gosh!" Jazz said. "Look!"

A crowd of kids had gathered at our playground's chain-link fence. Across the street, a white van was parked next to Grandma. It said, CHANNEL 8 NEWS—OUR NOSE KNOWS NEWS.

We ran to the fence to hear what the reporter was saying.

"This is Tony Zhang for Channel 8 News. I'm here on Sixth Street in downtown Bentley, where well-known resident and activist Daisy Glover is chained to this bent yet massive tree, which is scheduled to be cut down Monday and replaced with a swimming-pool complex. Mrs. Glover, tell us what you hope to accomplish."

"I'm wantin' folks to realize the importance of our native American trees. This is an American elm. I've named him Elmer. He's one of Bentley's oldest livin' residents, over one hundred years old, and he's about to be chopped down—brutally murdered—all for the sake of ten parkin' spaces. *Ten lousy parkin' spaces!*"

The reporter looked into the camera. "Will the city council change its mind and let Elmer live? Or is Elmer destined to become firewood? This is Tony Zhang reporting live for Channel 8 News, where our nose knows news."

All the kids at the fence turned to look at me.

"Is that old lady *really* your grandma?"

"Why does she wear pink high-tops?"

"Does she like being chained to trees?"

I bit my lip. "Well, Grandma is . . . you see she actually . . ." I felt like a bug under a microscope. "What I'm trying to say is . . ." But I had no idea what I was trying to say.

Jazz put her arm over my shoulder. "What Annie's *trying* to say is that her grandma is a modern-day, ultra-licious hero. You know, like Martin Luther King, Junior. Eleanor Roosevelt. Lady Godiva."

"Ja-azz," I whispered. "Lady Godiva took a dare to ride her horse naked through the streets of town in order to lower taxes."

"And look what she got," Jazz said. "Lower taxes!"

Now everyone *really* stared and was probably wondering where in the world we had heard such a crazy story. Obviously, they hadn't skipped to the "Myths and Legends" section in the back of our world history book like Jazz and I had.

"Is your grandma one of those tree huggers from the sixties?"

"Is she planning to sleep out there?"

"I saw a guy on TV who ate tree bark. Does your grandma eat tree bark, too?"

Rather than crawl into a deep, dark hole never to show my face in public again, I opted for the next best thing—a fake bellyache.

"Um, I don't feel very good," I said, rubbing my belly and trying to look sick. "I think I'm going to throw up."

"Step back, people," Jazz said, giving me more space. "If she blows her cork, you don't want it landing on you."

"Eww, gross!"

"Is she gonna hurl?"

I covered my mouth. "I better, um, go to the nurse's office."

"I'll go with you, girlfriend."

"No, thanks," I told Jazz. And I hurried inside.

The nurse wasn't in, but her door was wide open so I helped myself to her phone.

"Bentley First State Bank," Mom said. "How may I help you?"

"Mom?" I said, trying to sound sick. *Cough. Cough.* "I don't feel good. My belly aches. My head hurts." *Cough. Cough.* "I think I'm going to throw up. Can you come get me?"

"Annie, we already discussed this at breakfast this morning. Now I know today's a difficult day, but I can't take off work just because you're embarrassed over Grandma."

"But, Mo-om. I'm really sick and I can prove it." *Cough. Cough.* "See? I'm not faking! And I'm about to throw up any second."

"Sweetie, I know you're not sick. Now I get off at three o'clock, so I'll see you when you get home. Just try to ignore Grandma and pretend she's not even there. Bye!"

I plunked down the phone. *Easy for her to say.*

"Annie-Glover's-a-tree-lover. Annie-Glover's-a-tree-lover."

I sat on Bus 40 with my head against the window. It was only a ten-minute ride home, but because of Leroy it felt like an eternity.

I closed my eyes and covered my ears. Then Leroy scooted over to my seat, inched under my skin like the tick that he was, and said it even louder.

"Annie-Glover's-a-tree-lover!"

I had had enough. "Oh yeah? Well, Leroy Kirk's a . . . a skinny little jerk! How do you like *those* apples?"

Apparently he didn't, because he sulked back to his own seat.

Finally, the bus stopped at my corner and I quickly made my way down the aisle and stepped off.

Click. Slide.

A window opened. Out popped Leroy's red head.

"Annie-Glover's-a-treeeeeeeeeeeee-loverrrrrrrrrrrr!"

THE BEDROOM STINKER-
UPPERS ARE COMING!

Uh-huh . . . of course! Yes, we're, um, *thrilled* you're coming to visit!"

I walked into the kitchen and poured myself a glass of chocolate milk, listening to Mom talk on the phone. I could tell by the tone of her voice that she wasn't actually thrilled about whoever was coming to visit.

DD, our tiny apricot poodle, ran in circles, yapping around my feet and pulling my shoelaces.

Mom waved her hand, motioning us to be quiet.

"We'd *love* to have you . . . *Really*. No problem . . . Oh, you're bringing Walt and Jaroslav with you, too?"

I choked and almost spit milk out my nose. That could only be one person. *Uncle Claude.* Uncle Claude was an Elvis impersonator. So were his buddies, Walt and Jaroslav. Walt and Uncle Claude were old friends from high school. They met Jaroslav at a parachuting convention in the Czech Republic a few years ago. They started talking, realized they were all devout Elvis fanatics, and next thing you know, they went into business together.

They call themselves the Flying Elvis Trio and parachute from airplanes in white, diamond-studded Elvis costumes for grand openings and other events. They also sing like Elvis. Kind of. Well, not really, but *they* like to think so. You'd be surprised at how much business they get.

Mom held the phone with one hand and pretended to choke herself with the other. "Tomorrow night? Okay, little brother, we'll see you then. Bye!" She plunked down the phone and took a long, sad sip of my chocolate milk. "Bad news," she said. "Uncle Claude's coming to visit. He's bringing Walt and Jaroslav, too."

"Does this mean I have to give up my room and sleep on the sofa again?"

Mom nodded. "Two of them can sleep on your bunk bed and one on the rollaway."

"Mo-om! Why can't they sleep in the garage?

Or how about the shed? The shed would be a good place to put them."

Mom ruffled my hair. "They can't sleep in the garage or the shed and you know it. That's no way to treat family."

"But those three never leave. They eat up all of Dad's Nutty Buddy Chocolate Swirl ice cream and you know how Dad feels about that ice cream."

Mom couldn't argue with me there. Dad had a thing for Nutty Buddy Chocolate Swirl. Nobody messed with his Nutty Buddy. Not even me or Mom. We had to keep our own separate carton because he didn't like to share.

"Those three say, 'Thank you, thank you very much!' a million-zillion times. They leave their peel-and-stick sideburns all over the bathroom mirror. And worse yet, they *fart* in my bed!"

"Now how do you know that?"

"I can hear them—*even on the sofa!*"

Mom laughed. "It's only for a few days, sweetie."

"That's what you said last time, and it ended up being a whole month. A *whole month* of flying, farting Elvises."

DD jumped into my lap, trying to sniff my chocolate milk. DD stood for Dirty Dog because he always managed to get outside, roll in the mud, and walk around with sticks and dried grass in his fur.

"This is great, just great," I said. "Uncle Claude and his buddies think they're Elvis. Grandma chains herself to trees. Mom, why can't our family be normal? I'd even settle for *halfway* normal."

"We're normal. Kind of."

"Mo-om. Even our *dog* isn't normal. Look at him—he's got grass coming out his ears. There's something definitely wrong here."

"That's how families are, sweetie. You take what you get—Elvis lovers, tree lovers, dirty dogs, and all. Besides, you know how Grandma is."

"Do you know what she put me through today?" I asked. "Everybody kept staring at me like I was some kind of freak. They kept asking stupid, embarrassing questions like 'Does your grandmother chain herself to telephone poles, too?' And 'How does your grandma pee out there?' Then all the way home on the bus I had to listen to 'Annie-Glover's-a-tree-lover-Annie-Glover's-a-tree-lover.' "

"I'm sorry, sweetie," Mom said, giving me a hug.

"I'm *not* a tree lover. I'm a swimming-pool lover. And a Bahama Mama snow cone lover. I hate that stupid ol' tree."

"Oh, Annie, you don't mean that."

"I do, and I hope they chop it down."

"But I love that tree," Mom said. "I used to play in that vacant lot when I was a kid. And so did your father."

"I know and I've played there, too. But I can find somewhere else to play. It doesn't have to be under *that* tree."

"You two are not going to believe this!" Dad beamed at dinnertime, which clued me in to the fact that Mom hadn't told him yet about Uncle Claude and his buddies coming to stink up my room tomorrow night.

"I got it. I finally got the promotion! You're now looking at the new district sales manager of Aunt Bessie's Frozen Chili Dogs and More."

"Oh, honey, that's wonderful," Mom said. "I'm proud of you!"

Dad looked at me. "Well? What do *you* think?"

"I think this is the most humiliating thing Grandma has ever done," I said, forking a piece of chicken onto my plate. "Pass the fried okra, please."

Dad passed the fried okra. "I'm not talking about my mother, Annie. I'm talking about my promotion."

"I know, I know," I said. "But do you know how embarrassing she is? Dad, why does she have to do this crazy stuff? And right in front of my whole school!"

Dad shrugged. "Just be glad she wasn't *your* mother. When I was your age, she hauled me all over town fighting against you name it—spiraling health costs, illegal drug use, growing crime rates. Say, I've got a good idea. Why don't we celebrate my new promotion with a family camping trip this weekend? We could go to Beavers Bend Resort Park. Rent a cabin. Go hiking, fishing, even roast marshmallows. How about it?"

"Yeah, yeah!" I said. "And we can get a burger at the Eager Beaver Diner!"

Then Mom dropped the bomb.

"Speaking of this weekend," she said, putting down her fork. "I got a call from Claude today."

Dad's smile disappeared. "Oh no."

Mom nodded.

"Is he coming to mooch off us again?"

"Not mooch—visit," Mom said.

"When?"

"Tomorrow. But only for a few days."

"A few days, more like one *month*!" Dad said. "That guy *never* leaves."

"He's coming with Walt and Jaroslav. They're doing a jump for Dino's Reliable Used Cars. It's their anniversary celebration."

"Terrific," Dad said. "Here we go with another invasion of the flying Elvis ding-dongs. If they come to the door wearing those stupid white capes again, I'm not answering it. And another thing, I'm hiding my Nutty Buddy Chocolate Swirl in the back of the freezer. Last time those three devoured my whole carton in ten minutes flat."

Mom started laughing. "Poor little boy. Did those big, bad Elvis impersonators eat up all your ice cream?" She ruffled Dad's hair, causing the long strand he used to cover his bald spot to stand up straight, making his head look like a lowercase letter *d*.

"Well, they *did*," he said, smoothing down his hair. "Pass the chicken."

• • •

After dinner, we sat in the den, watching the six o'clock news on Channel 8. Apparently everyone else in Bentley was watching it, too, because after they showed Grandma's interview the phone wouldn't stop ringing.

"Oh yes!" Mom said to one caller. "We're *very* proud of her."

Easy for Mom to say. She didn't have to answer a million-trillion stupid dumb questions from every fourth-grader in Will Rogers Elementary.

"You know how Daisy is," she said to another caller. "She really stands up for what she believes in."

"That's for sure," Dad told someone else. "My mother's definitely a mover and a shaker. What? Oh no, I leave all that up to her. She's the radical one of the family."

When the news was over and I was ready to crawl into a hole and eat worms, Mom told me to slip on my shoes and go get Grandma.

"Mo-om!"

"Don't Mom me, young lady. Now bring her on home or she'll stand out there all night long and freeze her fanny off. And take DD for a walk while you're at it."

• • •

Passing pumpkins on porches and dogs racing
DD from behind their fences, we made our way
through the crisp night air to go get Grandma.

Four blocks and one turn later, I stood in the
shadows, watching Grandma wave her sign and
shout into her bullhorn.

A lime green pickup truck slowed, as if the
driver were reading the sign, then continued on its
way.

I quickly dashed across the street, hoping I
could convince Grandma to leave with me before
anyone else happened to drive by.

"Hey, Grandma."

"Hi there, Chickadee."

"Mom told me to come get you or you'll
freeze your fanny off. Are you ready to go?"

"Go? I'm not goin' anywhere."

"*Grand-ma!* It's dark. It's cold. Mom says I have
to bring you home."

"I can't leave Elmer. He needs me."

"Aren't you hungry by now?"

Grandma rubbed her eyes. "Well, I am hungry.
I'm awfully tired, too."

"Come on then."

She looked thoughtful for a minute, then

handed me the key from her coat pocket. "I guess you're right. I'll come back first thing in the mornin'. A good night's sleep and a hot meal will do me good."

I turned the key in the padlock and *click*, Grandma was free.

She bent down, rubbing her ankles. "Woo-wee, my achin' feet! I've been standin' for so long they've gone to sleep."

While Grandma was hunched over, I grabbed Bo-Bo Stinker Pot and stuffed him inside my coat. If she was coming back out here tomorrow, that was her business. But Bo-Bo was *my* business and he wasn't coming with her.

Grandma stood up with a groan. Then we gathered her things and slowly headed for home.

Walking along through the wind-scattered leaves, I smelled the crisp fall air.

"You know, Chickadee, it sure feels good to give somethin' back to this tree after all it's given us. Just think, Elmer has been givin' to this community for over a hundred years without ever askin' for anything in return."

I stared at Grandma. "I don't know what you're talking about. Trees don't give us anything. Unless you want to count *embarrassment*!"

"Sure they do. Why, every single time you take a breath, you can thank a tree for all the oxygen it gives you."

I wasn't impressed.

"They give shade on a sunny day and protection from wind. They give fruit to eat and juice to drink. You know those Bahama Mama snow cones you like so much?"

I nodded.

"They're made with coconut flavorin'. Guess where coconuts come from?"

I knew but I didn't want to admit it.

"Did you know trees are like animal hotels? Just think of all the animals and insects that live in and on trees."

"Maybe. But I'd *still* rather have a pool. You can't swim in a tree, Grandma. I've got you there and you know it."

Grandma laughed. "That's true, Chickadee."

"Us kids want that pool, Grandma. If you save that tree, we won't get our pool."

"Sure you will. The city council just needs to put their thinking caps on and figure out another place to put it."

"But if you mess things up, we may *never* get

our pool. They might decide it's too much trouble. I don't want that tree saved."

"Why, Annie Dawn Glover! I'm surprised at you. Elmer's trunk is over four feet in diameter. *Four feet!* I've had him tested for diseases and he's healthy as can be. In fact, when we're both dead and pushin' up daisies, guess who will still be here? Elmer. But only if we protect him."

The lime green pickup truck came by again. Only *this* time it drove right along beside us and a man with red cheeks leaned out the window.

"Hey, lady!" he shouted. "Why don't you mind your own business and leave that tree alone?"

Grandma jutted out her chin. "That tree *is* my business!"

"Oh yeah? Well, it's my business, too. I'm the guy the city hired to cut it down, and come Monday, you better get outta my way!"

He revved his motor, then sped off down the street, but not before I got a good look at the white lettering on his truck's door:

KIRK'S LANDSCAPING—
LET KIRK DO YOUR WORK

T-R-E-E-S

What's wrong, Annie-Fannie-Wannie?" Leroy asked the next day at school, pulling out three tissues from his travel-size box of Kleenex.

I *hated* when he called me that name.

"Last night my dad told me he's the one who's gonna cut down that tree. He said when he gets paid, he'll buy me the new pair of sneakers I've been wanting. They have electromagnetic fibers built into the soles and they're guaranteed to make me run fast. So *HA* on you!"

I laid my head down on my desk, covering it with my arm. Talking to Leroy was like talking to a fence post—useless.

"My dad said if your grandma doesn't get out of the way, he'll cut her in half."

I lifted up my elbow and peeked out. "He wouldn't dare."

"Would too." Leroy honked into his tissues, making a big, loud production of it, and then stuffed them in his pocket. "I saw his chain saw. It's real sharp. All I did was touch it and I started bleeding. Just think what it'll do to your crazy ol' grandma." Then he made a sound like a chain saw. *"Rem-rem-rem-rem-remmmmm!"*

For a fence post, he sure was annoying.

"Good morning, class," Mrs. Hodge said, walking into the room. She had coffee in one hand and a stack of papers in the other. Her hair had been pulled back with a white sash. "I want to remind everyone that today's our book fair. But for now, let's get out a clean sheet of paper and get ready to write."

Everyone moaned, including me.

Mrs. Hodge took a sip of her coffee. "Last night I saw Annie's grandmother on the news. I started thinking about her protest and thought this would be a good opportunity for us to write an essay."

On the board, in big letters, she wrote: T-R-E-E-S.

"Today we have a tree across the street that's in danger of being cut down," she said.

Leroy popped up from his chair and over to the window. "Mrs. Hodge! Mrs. Hodge! My—"

"Leroy, sit back down."

"But my dad—"

"Now."

He sat down, and Mrs. Hodge continued, "I want everyone to write an essay about trees. Maybe you can write about a time you climbed a tree. Or a time you fell *out* of a tree. Maybe you have a tree house. I want everyone to write about a special tree in your life."

Leroy's hand popped up and so did he. "Mrs. Hodge! Mrs. Hodge! What if we don't have a special tree? What if we don't even like trees? What if we hate trees' guts?"

"Leroy, trees do not have guts. If you get out of your chair one more time, you're headed to the office." Then to the rest of the class, she said, "If you don't have a special tree to write about, then write how you feel about trees. Do you like them? Why? Do you hate them? Why?"

Leroy's hand shot up, but this time he stayed in his chair. "Mrs. Hodge! Mrs. Hodge! What if I'm allergic to trees? What if they make my eyes swell and my ears ache and my nose—"

Mrs. Hodge pointed to the North Pole, a table in the back of the room covered with photos of Arctic explorers and maps of the Arctic region. It served as a "cooldown" zone for four-letter-word users, mean ol' copycatters, and sneaky crayon nabbers. In Leroy's case, it was for chair popper outers, teacher sassers, interrupters, and plain ol' meanies, which meant Leroy was probably an Arctic expert by now.

He stomped to the North Pole, taking his travel-size box of Kleenex and his emergency medical kit with him.

"Class? You may begin writing your essays. When you're finished, be sure to proofread, and then raise your hand if you want to read your essay out loud."

For the next half hour, we busied ourselves writing about trees. Then, one by one, hands shot up all over the room.

Mrs. Hodge called on Dave Goldberg first. Dave was the cutest boy in class, and all the girls liked him because he had long eyelashes and a nice, wide smile that looked like it belonged in a magazine or a toothpaste commercial.

"I have a tree house in my backyard," Dave read. "One time I got my Great Dane, Snoopy, to go up the ladder by putting pieces of liver on every step. It was really funny to see him climbing the ladder, but when he reached the top, he was afraid to come back down. No matter how hard we tried, he wouldn't budge. He howled and howled. Mom had to call the fire department to help him down, and I had to do the dishes for four days in a row!"

More kids read. They read about raking leaves into big golden piles and jumping into them. About finding nests with newborn, fuzzy-headed baby birds that looked like little Einsteins inside. They read about picking cherries and making cherry pie and being tricked into eating sour persimmons by mean ol' cousins and helping sell Christmas trees with their Boy Scout troops.

"Once I sailed the Dead Sea in a pirate ship," Martin read. "I discovered a treasure chest buried under a palm tree. Inside were gold coins, rubies, and a necklace made of ancient shrunken heads."

Martin had what Mrs. Hodge called a "vivid imagination" but what the rest of us called a "weird personality." He was always going around wearing an eye patch, insisting we call him by his pirate name, Nitram, which was just his real name spelled backward, and chasing us girls at recess saying *"ARRRRR!"* and *"Ahoy, matey!"*

"Thank you, Martin," Mrs. Hodge said. "That was, uh, quite a work of fiction, wasn't it?"

"Pirates like me never write fiction," Martin said. "We live lives of mayhem and adventure wherever we go."

"I *see*," Mrs. Hodge said. She looked around the room, and when no one else volunteered to read, she tapped on the side of her nose. "Hmm . . . I think this is a good time to share a book. Let's all move to the reading rug."

Everyone scrambled to the reading rug. It was just a piece of orange shag carpet that Mrs. Hodge had bought at a garage sale, but everyone loved it. Sometimes she passed around a tray of her famous homemade chocolate-chip cookies that were so out of this world delicious they made our mouths drool.

"The book I'm going to read is a classic," Mrs. Hodge said. She got out her tray, which meant we were in luck—today was cookie day. We knew to take only one each and to pass the tray to Leroy last because one time he got it first and licked all the cookies so nobody else would want them. Mrs. Hodge was so mad she made him sit at the North Pole for the rest of the day and banned him from the rug for the rest of the week.

"This book is called *The Giving Tree* and is

written by Shel Silverstein. It's about a tree who loves a boy so much, it gives everything it has to the boy, even its very life."

We listened, munching our cookies, letting the chocolaty goodness melt on our tongues, and as the pages turned, my eyes began to fill with tears at the plight of that poor tree.

"Look at this book. It's glorious. And this one. It's ultra-glorious!"

I stepped back to examine the book Jazz was holding in front of my eyes at the book fair. It was another one of those horse books with a horse necklace attached. I wasn't interested.

"How about this one?" Jazz asked, holding up a different book as though she were my own personal saleslady. "Or *this* one?"

"No, thanks. I'm thinking about buying a dog poster. Or maybe one of these diaries." I showed her a locking diary that came with a key and a purple gel pen.

Dave Goldberg thumbed through a book of presidential trivia. "Hey, listen to this," he said. "Ulysses S. Grant once got a speeding ticket and a twenty-dollar fine for riding his horse too fast."

Jazz and I laughed.

Jazz ended up buying a hairstyle book that came with hair beads and instructions to make ten different glamour-girl hairstyles and a little blue paperback entitled *Name That Town*. All the illustrations were plain ol' black-and-white photographs, and it looked completely boring.

"Why'd you buy *that* book?" I asked.

"Annie-Ba-Nannie! Why this book is grandtastic. Look—it's about towns and how they got their names. I'll bet it's full of totally tragic stories. Maybe even some deliciously romantic ones, too."

I should have known she'd pick a book like that, since totally tragic and deliciously romantic history was her favorite subject.

I rummaged around a little longer, finally choosing a pink, strawberry-scented eraser, a pen with ten different colors of ink, and a nonfiction book about sea turtles.

The cafeteria was filled with the smell of hamburgers and French fries. I took a sip of milk and shook my lunch sack upside down—a bologna sandwich with no cheese, an apple that had seen better days, and three graham crackers with chocolate coating. Before I could even unwrap my sandwich, my whole entire class crowded around me.

"I saw your grandma on the news last night."

"My mom said your grandma has marbles in her head."

"Does she chain herself to rosebushes? 'Cause rosebushes have thorns and that would hurt."

"When does she eat?"

I took another sip of my milk. How was *I* supposed to know when she ate? I bit into my apple so I wouldn't have to answer.

"My dad said if she was smart, she'd chain a sofa to the tree so she could lay on it!"

"My big sister who's in college said your grandma's a weirdo. My big sister knows about weirdos because she used to date this guy who could turn his eyelids inside out."

"Well, I think Annie's grandma is brave," Dave Goldberg said.

"Me, too," Jazz said. "She's a modern-day, ultra-licious hero. Isn't that right, Annie?"

I cleared my throat, embarrassed at all the attention. "My grandma's really not a hero," I managed to say. Then I cupped my hand over Jazz's ear. "Ja-azz, don't you think you're going a little overboard again?"

"No I'm not, girlfriend. Your grandma *is* a modern-day, ultra-licious hero."

My cheeks felt flushed.

"Um, I, uh . . . I think I need some water," I said. But instead of rushing to the water fountain, I made my way to the nurse's office and once again borrowed her phone. Maybe if I begged and pleaded, this time Mom would come get me.

"Bentley First State Bank," Mom said. "How may I help you?"

"Mom? Please-*come-get-me*-I'll-do-anything-I'll-wash-the-dishes-I'll-vacuum-the-house-I'll-keep-my-room-spotless-for-the-rest-of-my-life-just-come-get-me-*please*?"

"Sweetie, as much as I'd like to take you up on your generous offer, I can't come get you."

"This is so humiliating. *Pleeeeaaaassse?* I'll clean the garage and give DD a bath. You know how badly he needs a bath."

"True," Mom said, sighing. "I'm really sorry you have to deal with this. But believe me, it's not easy for your dad and me, either. I've already had several customers come in today asking if I'd seen the *kooky tree lady* . . . Sweetie, the other line is ringing and I've got to go. I'll see you after school. Hang in there."

I thunked down the phone. *So much for begging and pleading.*

• • •

"Quit it!" I said. Staring out the window of Bus 40, I rolled my pink, strawberry-scented eraser round and round in my fist.

But Leroy didn't quit. "Annie-Glover's-a-tree-lover. Annie-Glover's-a-treeee-loverrrrr."

I covered my ears and hummed real loud, trying to drown him out. But he kept on saying it, over and over.

When the bus stopped at my corner, I shot out of my seat and stepped off.

Click. Slide.

A window opened.

I smiled secretly because this time I was prepared.

"Annie-Glover's-a—"

Donk! My pink, strawberry-scented eraser hit Leroy smack in the middle of his puny little forehead.

"Hey! I'm tellin' on you!"

"Go ahead, you little tattletale baby!"

Then the bus drove out of sight, taking mean ol' Leroy with it.

INVASION OF THE FLYING ELVIS DING-DONGS

That night at dinner, Mom heated chili dogs in the microwave, and added mustard, onions, and cheese.

"Mmm, these are good," I said, licking chili off my pinkie. I never got tired of the countless boxes of chili dogs Dad brought home from work. Good thing for me he didn't work at a place that sold frozen Brussels sprouts!

"So did your day get any better?" Mom asked.

"All day long it was *Grandma, Grandma, Grandma*. Even the lunch ladies and the custodian were talking about her."

Dad laughed. "Oh well . . . it'll all be over soon. Come Monday morning they'll either cut down the tree or leave it. I sure hope they leave it, though. I like that old tree."

"Me, too," Mom said, pouring iced tea in our

glasses. "Say, honey-bunch, remember the first time you kissed me? It was under that tree." They both started smiling and nudging each other. Then Dad leaned over and gave Mom a big smooch on the lips.

Yuck!

"Do you remember me carving our initials onto that tree?" Dad asked.

"I sure do," Mom said. "Elmer's seen a lot of initials in his day, hasn't he?"

Elmer was so carved up with initials and hearts that if you looked hard enough, you'd find practically everyone in Bentley.

I thought about my own memories of Elmer. Like all the times I'd played hide-and-seek on that vacant lot, using Elmer as home base. And how I'd played flashlight tag there a million-zillion times. And caught lightning bugs beneath Elmer's drooping branches. Last summer, I caught a whole jarful and let them go in my bedroom so I could watch them blink all night. Mom wasn't too happy about that.

"Hey, remember the time Jazz and I climbed up Elmer and we sat there reading our library books for so long and you didn't know where we were?"

Mom leaned her head back and laughed. "How could I forget? I was so worried because one minute you two were in the front yard, and just like that, you disappeared. I combed the entire neighborhood, knocking on every door. Jazz's mom is the one who suggested looking in Elmer, and when we finally found you two, we didn't know whether to hug you or spank you."

"You did both," I said. "And you didn't let me play with Jazz for a solid week."

"You know," Dad said, passing the salad. "I still say we should take off for Beavers Bend this weekend."

Mom eyed Dad. "We can't go away and leave Claude here unsupervised. This place would be a wreck!"

"Yeah, I guess you're right," Dad grumped.

"So when are Uncle Claude and his buddies going to get here?" I asked.

Mom shrugged. "With those three, there's no telling. Remember that time they showed up at two in the morning?"

"How could I forget?" Dad said. "They woke up half the neighborhood honking their Viva Las Vegas horn until we got up and let them in."

Ding-dong-ding-dong-ding-dong-ding-dong-ding-dong-ding-dong!

DD took off for the front door barking, and we all stared at each other with open mouths.

"Oh no!" Dad said. "The Elvis invasion is here. Quick, hide the ice cream!"

Mom tightened her lips. "Randolph, we'll do no such thing."

Tiptoeing into the living room, I lifted a corner of the curtain and peeked out.

"They better not be wearing those goofy white capes again," Dad said.

"They're wearing them," I said. "But this time they have something strange on their heads. Looks like . . . like dead raccoons."

"Dead raccoons?" Dad put his eye over the peephole and took a look for himself. Then he shook his head and started laughing. "Those goofballs are wearing coonskin caps. Whoever heard of Elvis in a coonskin cap?" He took another peek. "Great . . . they're still driving that oil-leaking, rattletrap of a junk heap. Don't they know that thing is an eyesore?"

"You mean the Elvis Mobile?"

Dad nodded.

The Elvis Mobile was a beat-up, run-down Chevy van that Uncle Claude had bought on eBay. The windshield was cracked and held together with silver tape. One door was green, and the others were the color of rust. Or maybe they *were* rust. It was hard to tell. Painted on the hood in pink and black letters were the words ELVIS LIVES!

"That's it," Dad said. "We're not answering this door. And that's final."

"Shhh," Mom whispered. "They might hear you."

"Hear me?" Dad asked. "How could they possibly hear me when they're still ringing the doorbell?"

Ding-dong-ding-dong-ding-dong-ding-dong-ding-dong-ding-dong!

"Do I have to give up my bedroom again? Can't they sleep in the basement?"

Mom pointed at me and Dad with a threatening finger. "Look, you two. They're *not* sleeping in the basement. We're *not* going to Beavers Bend. Do you hear? We're going to treat Claude and his friends like family. We're going to be nice and friendly and happy. Now smile." Then she opened the door. "Claude! So nice to see you!"

"Hey there, Sis! You're lookin' good!" Uncle

Claude said, grabbing Mom and twirling her off the floor.

"Hey, Annie Girl!" He twirled me off the floor, too, tangling me up in his cape. "Just look at you—tall as a beanpole!"

Then he turned to Dad. "Rudolph, my man!"

"It's Ran-dolph."

He tried to twirl Dad, but Dad wasn't the twirly type so they just kind of stood there, slapping each other's backs. "Good to see you, Rudolph."

"It's Randolph. *Ran*-dolph."

"I know, I know. Just pullin' your chain, man," Uncle Claude said. "You remember my best buds, my aces from outer spaces, my dudes with attitudes, Walt and Jaroslav, don't you?"

"How could I possibly forget," Dad said.

Walt wore black-rimmed glasses that came to a point on each side. Jaroslav had hoop earrings and a tattoo that said ELVIS HAS LEFT THE BUILDING. They were both pretty unforgettable.

Walt shook Dad's hand. "Mr. Glover? Dude! Good to see you. You don't mind if we bunk here for a few days, do you?"

"Well, now that you mention it, we already had plans to go to Beavers—*ouch!* No, I don't mind. Come on in."

I looked at Mom, who was standing there smiling, hiding the fact that she'd just used her secret weapon—her ol' pinch-on-the-back-of-the-arm trick—to keep Dad from saying something she didn't want him to say.

Jaroslav gave Dad a high five. "Mr. Glof-fer, goode to see you."

"Thanks," Dad said. "How are things in the Czech Republic?"

"Goode, goode," Jaroslav replied. "Very cold. Mooch snow."

"We were just eating dinner," Mom said. "Would you like to join us?"

"Dude!" Uncle Claude said. "Does Elvis shake his pelvis?" Which I think meant yes because they all three took off running for the dining room.

Mom went into the kitchen, leaving Dad and me to fend for ourselves with the Elvises.

"So," Dad said, as we took our seats. "Have you guys been on the road much?"

"Sure," Uncle Claude said. "Just spent five days on the road."

"Yeah, dude," agreed Walt. "Broke *down* on the road. We lost our engine."

Dad and I exchanged glances. How can anyone

lose an engine? It wasn't like they could have misplaced it or anything.

Jaroslav pointed to his head. "Thatz when we get awesome coonskin capz. See?"

All three of them turned their heads from left to right, making their raccoon tails swing in unison. I could tell they'd been practicing.

"So how did you get those caps if you were broke down on the road?" Dad asked.

"We were out in the Rocky Mountains doing a parachute jump for the grand opening of a new Giddy Up Gas Mart," Walt said. "After we were done, the Elvis Mobile just happened to break down right in front of a museum that had all sorts of groovy old western stuff. We got 'em in the gift shop. You like 'em?"

"Uh, well," Dad faked a smile, and I did, too. Then, lucky for us, Mom walked in with a heaping platter of chili dogs so we didn't have to tell Uncle Claude that it looked like a raccoon crawled up on his head and died there.

"What do *you* think, Sis?" Uncle Claude asked Mom. "You like our caps?"

"Oh. Sure I do," Mom said. "They're really, uh, really something."

"Good, 'cause I've got two more for you and

Ran-dolph." Uncle Claude fished around inside a pocket of his cape, then brought out a sack and handed it to Mom.

"For me? Oh, Claude! You shouldn't have." Mom opened the sack and pulled the caps out by their tails. "You really, *really* shouldn't have." Her nose wrinkled and her lips scrunched, making her look the exact same way she did last week when our toilet overflowed.

"Go ahead, put them on. They'll keep your ears warm."

Mom slowly lifted the cap to her head and smiled.

Dad cracked up laughing. That is, until Uncle Claude made him put *his* cap on.

Then Uncle Claude handed me a sack that luckily was too small to contain a coonskin cap. "Go ahead and open yours, Annie Girl."

I was afraid to. Last time he gave me a gift, it was a bobble-head dog with sideburns that wore an Elvis costume and sang "You ain't nothin' but a hound dog."

I carefully opened the sack, holding it away from me in case something jumped out. Inside was a CD.

"It's our new Christmas album," Uncle Claude

said, turning it over to show me a picture of the three of them dressed in red Santa hats. "See? It's got fifteen Christmas favorites, including 'Grandma Got Run Over by a Reindeer.' "

"But Elvis never sang that song," I said.

"He does now!" Uncle Claude said.

Jaroslav pointed to another song. "And we sing 'I Want a Hippo-pot-moose for Chris-maz.' "

Oh brother!

"So what do you think, Annie Girl?"

"Gee, I . . . I *love* it. I can't wait to hear it."

"Dude!" Walt said. "No need to wait. Go put it on while we eat!"

So I put on the CD, and for the rest of our dinner, we listened to "Santa Bring My Baby Back" and "Blue Christmas." Surprisingly, they didn't sing too bad. But then, they didn't sing too good, either.

After dinner, the three flying Elvises unloaded all their things—seven suitcases, two duffel bags, and a box of wigs and sunglasses—while Mom filled them in on Grandma's latest cause.

"You mean she's out there now?" Uncle Claude asked. "Chained to a tree?"

Mom nodded.

"Whoa, man! Granny rocks! Dudes, let's go pick her up in the Elvis Mobile!"

As their van clink-clank-clunked out the driveway, I dashed down the hall to get my pillow. I may have had to give up my room, but there was no way I was going to give up my pillow and let them get Elvis drool all over it.

In a few minutes, Grandma returned looking even more frazzled than yesterday, though I wasn't sure if it was due to being chained to a tree for two days in a row or from having ridden in the Elvis Mobile.

Mom helped Grandma with her coat and then got her settled at the dining room table with a ham and cheese sandwich, some celery with peanut butter, and a hot cup of coffee.

"It must be nearly freezin' out there," Grandma said, warming her hands over the steam rising from her cup. Then she picked up her coffee and took a long sip. "Aah, this hits the spot. Claude? Where'd you get your driver's license? Out of a gum-ball machine?"

"Come on now, Groovy Granny," Uncle Claude teased. "I'm a good driver."

"Yeah, good at runnin' stop signs," Grandma said. She took a bite of her sandwich.

Pouring more coffee into Grandma's cup, Mom said, "Daisy, it really is too cold for you to be out there. I'm worried you'll catch pneumonia. Promise me you won't go back tomorrow morning."

"Why, I'll do no such thing. That's what that city manager, Mr. Castillo, said today, too. Can you believe he had the nerve to tell me I was too old to be so radical and I should go home?"

"Speaking of going home," Dad said, slapping Uncle Claude's back. "How long do you three plan to stay? I'm sure you have plenty of important things to do."

"Don't worry," Uncle Claude replied. "My dudes with attitudes and I have already discussed this. We believe there's nothing more important than being with family on the holidays. So we're staying right here with you for Thanksgiving and we won't take no for an answer."

"But Thanksgiving isn't for two more weeks," Dad said. "You mean to tell me—"

"Well, well," Mom said. "We're so, um, happy to hear that. Aren't we, Annie?"

"Yeah. Real happy."

Walt put his arm around Dad's shoulder. "We knew you'd be excited. It's the least we could do. And just wait till you taste my 'I'm So Lonesome I Could Cry' pie. I make it every Thanksgiving. Got the recipe from a cookbook at a gift shop near Graceland. It's one of the King's favorites."

"Say," Uncle Claude said. "That reminds me. Last time we were here, you had this lip-smacking ice cream that was chocolate with little bitty marshmallows and nuts."

Dad tried to act dumb. "Ice cream? No, I don't remember any ice cream."

"Sure you do," Mom said. "It was your Nutty Buddy Chocolate Swirl."

Uncle Claude's eyes lit up. "Yeah, dude! That was it. Got any more of that?"

Dad shot Mom a mean look. "Nope. We're fresh out. I ate it all up yester— *Ouch!* Okay. You can have some."

Mom got out the scoop and three bowls.

"No need to dirty up clean bowls just for us, Sis. Just give us spoons and me and my boys will eat right out of the carton. Won't we, boys?"

"But what about me?" Dad asked. "It's my ice cream. I want some, too."

"Just grab a spoon and dive in!" Uncle Claude said. "We don't mind sharing."

"No, thanks," Dad said. "I think I'll just get my own bowl."

After the three Kings of Rock-and-Roll scraped every last drop from the bottom of Dad's ice cream carton, and even licked the lid clean, everyone finally settled down for the night.

I wasn't sure who was more miserable, though—Dad, who was now completely out of his Nutty Buddy Chocolate Swirl, or me, having to sleep on the bumpy, lumpy sofa.

I tossed and turned, punching my pillow a million-kajillion times, listening to the *ticktock* of the clock, the humming of the refrigerator, and the farting of the Elvises.

Frrrt. FRT. FRR-RRT!

I covered my head with my pillow, but when I lifted it off, they were still at it. And one of them was farting in another language.

Frrt-z. FRT-Z. FRRRT-Z!

I sat up straight, remembering Bo-Bo. Poor Bo-Bo, stuck in there with those three bedroom stinker-uppers! So I tiptoed down the dark hallway and tapped on my door.

No answer. They probably couldn't hear me with all the noise they were making.

I tapped a little louder and whispered, "Pssst. Uncle Claude? I need something from my room."

The door opened an inch. "No more autographs, please."

"I don't want your autograph."

"You want an official fan club ID card? Hold on a second."

"I don't want an official fan club ID card. I just want my teddy bear. He's on my dresser. Can you get him?"

The door closed.

I could hear the three of them whispering and laughing. Then the door opened.

"Here." He shoved Bo-Bo into my arms.

"Thanks," I said and headed back down the dark hallway to the living room.

I settled onto the sofa, holding Bo-Bo under my chin, but my fingers felt something strange. Something fuzzy.

I sat up and clicked on the light.

Bo-Bo Stinker Pot had two furry, fake sideburns stuck on his chest.

I sighed. This was going to be a looooong night.

I had just fallen asleep when the phone next to the sofa rang.

I sat up, rubbing my eyes. It was 11:57 p.m. *Who would call this late?*

"Hello?"

"Annie-Ba-Nannie!"

"H-hello?" Dad said into the other extension.

"Dad? I've already got it. It's Jazz," I said.

"Jazz?" Dad asked. "What does she want this late at night?"

"I don't know," I said. "Jazz, what do you want this late at night?"

"Oh, Annie! You're not going to believe this. *I* can't even believe it."

"Dad? She says I'm not going to be—"

"I heard her," Dad said. "Girls? Can't this wait until tomorrow?"

"Sorry, Mr. Glover," Jazz said. "It'll only take a few minutes and it's really, *really* important."

"Okay, but make it snappy." Dad hung up the phone.

"What's up?" I asked.

"Well, remember the blue paperback I bought at the book fair today?"

"You mean that ol' boring one with black-and-white photographs?"

"Yeah, but it's not boring. It's fab, Annie. Like totally ultra. I couldn't put it down at bedtime, so

I've been reading with a flashlight under the covers. And you won't believe in a million years what I just learned. You know that bent tree your grandma—"

"Wait!" I said. "Is this another one of your deliciously romantic stories?"

I heard a little gasp.

"Look, Jazz. You've got to admit you go overboard with this totally tragic, deliciously romantic stuff. I mean, look at you, calling me in the middle of the night, for gosh sakes!"

The line was silent.

"Jazz?"

"I do not go overboard."

"You do too. And you keep romanticizing my grandma like she's some kind of a hero and she's not."

"She is too!"

"She is not!"

Click.

"Jazz? Hello? Hello?"

A TOTALLY, *TOTALLY* TRAGIC STORY

"Just look what you did with your eraser, Annie-Fannie-Wannie," Leroy said the next day at school. Snatching off his knit hat, he revealed a teeny-weeny black-and-blue bruise on his forehead. "I told my dad. So *HA* on you!"

He pressed a sandwich bag full of ice cubes to his forehead, acting as though I'd permanently injured his puny little head. "And my dad says if I have to go to the hospital over this, your dad's gonna pay the bill. So *double HA* on you! Now I'm gonna tell Mrs. Hodge. So *triple HA* on you!"

"Good morning, class," Mrs. Hodge said, smiling around the room. Her soft, red bangs had been swept back with a hair band, making her look every bit as pretty as one of those TV ladies who advertise laundry soap or oven cleaner.

After morning announcements and the Pledge

of Allegiance, Martin read the lunch menu with his eye patch on. "Spaghetti, salad, dinner roll, and *ARRRRR*tichokes."

Mrs. Hodge laughed. "Martin, take that eye patch off right now."

"But I'm a pirate and pirates *ARRRRR* supposed to wear eye patches."

"Not in *my* classroom. Now take that thing off."

Just as Martin sat down, Leroy popped out of his chair, waving his sandwich bag of ice cubes. "Mrs. Hodge! Mrs. Hodge! Yesterday after school, Annie threw a whole box of erasers at me and hit me in the forehead! Look!"

"I did not," I said. "I mean, I did, but it was only one little eraser."

"Was not!"

"Was too and you know it."

Mrs. Hodge raised an eyebrow. "Annie! Did you really make that bruise on his forehead?"

"Yes, but he kept singing over and over 'Annie-Glover's-a-tree-lover-Annie-Glover's-a—' "

"I didn't either. I never said that."

"You did too."

"Did not."

"Did too!" Now I was mad. Really mad.

"Mrs. Hodge! Just look at this huge bruise! My dad says I'm lucky she didn't put my eye out!"

I slammed my hand on my desk. "Quit exaggerating, Leroy Kirk!"

Mrs. Hodge clapped her hands. "Annie! Leroy! That's enough! I want *both* of you to go to the North Pole!"

I grabbed my pencil and headed to the North Pole with Leroy, Mr. Liar-Liar-Pants-on-Fire.

From the back of the room, I could see everyone in class. Jazz must have read her new glamour-girl hairstyle book because her hair had been swept up into a French twist with pink and yellow beads.

"Mrs. Hodge?" Jazz asked, standing up and covering her heart. "Can I tell the class a totally, *totally* tragic story?"

Oh brother! I slumped down in my seat.

"Yesterday at the book fair, I bought this ultra-fab paperback called *Name That Town*. Last night I was reading it in bed when I discovered something so big, so splen-dicious that I immediately phoned someone who I *thought* was my best friend, but she turned out to be a fake." She stopped talking and casually looked at me.

A fake? How dare that ol' meanie say I'm a fake?

I'm not a fake, she is. She's the one who hung up on me.

"What I discovered is this," Jazz continued. "The town of Bentley, *our* very own town, was originally named Bent Tree, but through the years it was changed to Bent-ley. And get this, it was named after an unusually shaped tree. Here's a photo taken back in 1907."

She opened the book and held it up.

The black-and-white photograph showed a tree. It was young and skinny with just a few scraggly limbs, but it was already bent and crooked.

"Oh my gosh!" I said, sitting straight up in my chair. "That's Elmer!"

Mrs. Hodge looked as shocked as the rest of us. "This certainly changes things, doesn't it?"

For the rest of the morning, I thought about Elmer. I thought about Grandma. As much as I hated to admit it, maybe Jazz was right. Maybe Grandma really *was* a hero.

At lunch, Jazz totally ignored me and sat next to Dave Goldberg.

I quickly surveyed my class's table, eyeing my available options.

Leroy Kirk? Absolutely not! I wouldn't sit with him if he was the only person in the cafeteria.

Dixie Lurken? No. I still hadn't forgiven her for blabbing to the whole class who Grandma was.

Martin? Well, maybe. He didn't look very inviting, though, with that eye patch on, but at least he was better than Leroy, who was sneezing all over his food and everyone else's.

I glanced around some more, feeling awkward. I didn't want Jazz to see me sitting alone, so Martin would have to do.

"Hi, Martin," I said. "Can I sit with you?"

"Step aboard!" he said, which I think meant yes. "Nitram's the name. Avoiding the plank's my game!"

What did I get myself into? I started to move, but when I looked over at Jazz, she was watching me, so I quickly sat down, acting like Martin and I were the best of buds.

"So." I couldn't think of a single thing to say. "Um . . . did you get a book at the book fair yesterday?"

Martin eyed me suspiciously. "Yeah. I got the pirate book that came with a secret treasure map decoder ring."

I emptied my lunch sack—a cheese sandwich,

an orange, a piece of Dad's homemade beef jerky, and two deviled eggs.

"*ARRRRR* you gonna eat those deviled eggs?" Martin asked. "Nitram will trade with you."

I inspected his lunch to see if he had anything worth trading for—milk, a peanut butter sandwich that already had a bite taken out of it, a cream-filled cupcake that looked like someone had sat on it, a can of pork and beans, and a can opener.

"Martin, I mean, *Nitram*, why do you have a can of pork and beans in your lunch?"

" 'Cause pirates *like* pork and beans. We eat 'em right outta the can. We open the cans with our bare teeth—but my mom won't let me so I have to use a can opener."

"O-*kaaay*," I said. Scooting down the table a few inches, I made a quick mental note. *Use Dixie as backup friend number one and move Martin to number two.*

I looked at Jazz. There she was, all smiley and perky, sitting with the cutest boy in class, who had long eyelashes and a perfect magazine smile, while I was stuck with a pirate wannabe who had nothing but a stupid can of pork and beans and a dumb patch over his eye.

Dave pulled out his new presidential trivia

book and started thumbing through it. "Did you know teddy bears were named after Teddy Roosevelt? And listen to this, Dwight D. Eisenhower's dog was banned from the White House because it pooped and peed on the floor!"

"That's *sooo* funny," Jazz said, giving me a sideways glance.

Dave went on reading. "More presidents were born in Virginia than in any other state . . . Andrew Jackson had a pet parrot who could talk and cuss. It cussed so much during Jackson's funeral, it had to be taken away!"

"Oh, Dave," Jazz said, glancing my way again. "You're fun-tastic. We should sit together more often."

If Jazz was doing this just to make me jealous, it was definitely working.

Martin took a loud, slurpy sip of his milk. "Pirates drink rum off a dead man's chest—but my mom says I've gotta drink milk from a carton."

I didn't respond. I mean, how do you respond to *that*?

"Did I ever tell you about the time a band of women pirates captured me in the Red Sea, held me prisoner, and forced me to eat an alligator carcass?"

"Um . . . no. I don't think you did." I scooted down the table a few more inches. Surely making up with Jazz would be easier than listening to Martin discuss dead men's chests and alligator carcasses, so I swallowed my pride and decided to give it a try.

"Jazz?"

"Dave, will you please tell Annie I'm *not* speaking to her?"

"Annie, Jazz isn't speaking to you," he repeated.

"Then would you ask her to *pleeeease* forgive me?" I begged, even though she was the one who went overboard, it was completely her fault, and I did nothing wrong.

"Jazz, would you *pleeeease* forgive her?" he repeated.

"Dave, will you tell her *only* if she takes back what she said on the phone last night?"

"Annie, Jazz said only if you—"

"I know what she said," I told Dave. I didn't like having a middleman. "Okay—I take back what I said on the phone last night."

"Dave, will you tell Annie—"

"That's enough of this!" he said. Picking up his trivia book and his lunch tray, he moved to the end of our table, leaving Jazz and me to fend for ourselves.

Jazz crossed her arms. "Tell me what you said on the phone that you're sorry for."

"Wait a minute," I said. "What about *me*? Aren't you going to tell me *you're* sorry?"

"Sorry for what?"

"For calling me a fake."

"Well, *you* said I go overboard."

"*You* hung up on me."

"Stop *ARRRRRguing*," Martin said, "or I'll make you *both* walk the plank!" Then he cranked open his can of pork and beans and poured the entire contents into his mouth, letting bean juice dribble down his neck.

I looked at Jazz. She looked at me. *Disgusting!*

"Listen, Jazz. I'm sorry for saying you take that totally tragic, deliciously romantic stuff overboard, even though you do."

"I'm sorry for hanging up on you, even though you wouldn't recognize a totally tragic, deliciously romantic story if it bit you in the behind."

Then we shook on it, rather grudgingly, but at least we shook on it, which meant I wasn't stuck sitting with Martin the bean eater anymore.

We ate our lunches, gathering our thoughts.

"I've been thinking about Elmer." I told Jazz.

"Me, too."

I peeled my orange, popping a slice into my mouth. "I can't believe Bentley is named after him."

"Me, neither," Jazz said.

"You know, if they cut down Elmer, I'd kind of sort of miss him. Hey, do you remember the time we climbed up Elmer to read our library books and—"

"—And our mothers were looking all over town for us," Jazz said, "and we weren't allowed to—"

"—Play together for an entire week?" we both said at the same time, smiling.

Jazz covered her heart and looked real serious. "Girlfriend, if Elmer's cut down and replaced by a pool, do you know what this means? No more hide-and-seek there."

"No more catching lightning bugs there, either."

I took another bite of orange and slowly chewed it, thinking. "Oh my gosh!"

"Oh my gosh *what*?"

"Do you know where DD was the very first time I saw him?"

"No way."

"Yes way," I said. "The pet adoption agency had set up a couple of booths under Elmer trying to get people to adopt homeless pets. He was sitting in a little cage, looking up at me with those sad brown eyes and a piece of grass stuck to his nose."

"Aaaw."

A lump jumped into my throat. "Jazz, are you thinking what I'm thinking?"

"What are you thinking?"

"That we can't let the city council do this. Pool or no pool, Bentley needs Elmer. For gosh sakes, he gave our town its name!"

Jazz gasped. "It's just like the book Mrs. Hodge read to us. *The Giving Tree*."

"Elmer's *our* giving tree," I said. "We can't let him end up like the tree in that book did. We better do something. Fast."

LEAF OUR TREE ALONE

Back in class, through a series of top secret notes passed under our desks, Jazz and I came up with a plan to save Elmer.

Her final note said,

Do you think it'll work?

I wrote back,

Maybe. Let's see what everyone else thinks.

So at the end of the day, during our individual reading time, we decided to ask Mrs. Hodge if we could share our plan with the class.

"Sure," Mrs. Hodge said, putting down her book and smiling. "I'm glad to see you two taking an interest in that tree. Class? Annie and Jazz have something they want to say."

Nervously, Jazz and I stood up in front of the room.

"We've been thinking a lot about Elmer," I said, shifting from one foot to the other. "And we, um, we've decided to help save him." I took a deep breath and looked around at my classmates. So far, no one was laughing. That was a good sign. "So we're wondering if you'd like to help us. Since tomorrow's Saturday, we thought we'd meet up at the tree, bring some signs, and—"

"Protest," Jazz said. "Isn't it fab? Like ultra-glorious? I mean, how often do us kids get to *protest*?"

Eyebrows went up all over the room.

"But what about the swimming pool?"

"Yeah, I want that pool!"

"And that high dive!"

"Me, too!"

"We *all* want that," I said. "But Grandma says there must be other places the city council can put the swimming pool. She says it's just a matter of changing their minds."

"So we'll still get our pool?"

"What about the snack bar?"

"And the snow cones?"

"Yes," Jazz said. "We'll have the entire glorious complex, just somewhere else." She covered her heart. "Can't you just see it now . . . Lone students . . . marching around Elmer with Annie's grandma . . . standing up for justice . . . working together to preserve history!"

Mrs. Hodge cleared her throat. "You know, the more I think about this, the more I realize it might not be a bad idea. In fact, it might even be a hands-on educational experience."

"Good," I said. "Because we'll need your help if we're going to do this."

Leroy popped up from his chair. "I think this is a stupid plan because my dad's already been hired to cut down that tree on Monday morning. And when he gets paid I'm getting new shoes with electromagnetic fibers built into the soles guaranteed to make me run fast. And I really want to run fast. Besides, I want that pool so I can go swimming this summer."

"We'll get the pool," I said, and the class cheered. Then under my breath, I added, "I hope."

Mrs. Hodge tapped her nose, thinking. "It *does*

tie in to the state history unit we're starting next week."

"So will you help us make some signs?" Jazz asked Mrs. Hodge. "Please?"

Mrs. Hodge looked out the window at Grandma. Then at us. Then at her watch. "Okay—but—we only have thirty minutes till the bell rings, so we better hurry. Class? I want everyone to get out your art supplies. Annie? Jazz? You two go to the art room and ask for some poster board and paint stirring sticks."

In a few minutes, Jazz and I returned with our arms full.

"Class? You can staple your poster board to the paint stirring stick like this." Mrs. Hodge stapled one to show us. "See? Now you have a sign with a handle. Make the letters extra-large so people driving down the street will be able to read them. Now, let's brainstorm for what our signs should say. Any suggestions?"

"Save our native tree!"

"Good," Mrs. Hodge said, writing it on the dry-erase board. "What else?"

"Trees rock!"

"Shiver me timbers!"

"Trees are ultra-fab-icent!"

"Great," Mrs. Hodge said. "Anything else?"

"Trees are tree-mendous!"

"Leaf our tree alone!"

"Down with trees!"

Mrs. Hodge looked at Leroy. "Leroy? You're free to voice your own opinion about Elmer. Go ahead and put that on your sign if that's really how you feel."

For the next twenty minutes, we busied ourselves coloring, stapling, glittering, and Magic-Markering while Mrs. Hodge wrote a letter to our parents to tell them what we were doing and made copies for us to take home.

"Now remember," Mrs. Hodge said, just before the bell rang. "Even though tomorrow's a Saturday, you're still representing our school. So no horsing around. You must conduct yourselves as ladies and gentlemen. Is that understood?"

"Yes, Mrs. Hodge!"

Dixie raised her hand. "What time should we meet at the tree tomorrow?"

"How many of you think you can meet at nine o'clock?" Mrs. Hodge asked.

Almost everyone's sign shot up in the air, even Leroy's.

"Nine it is!" Mrs. Hodge said.

I tapped Leroy on the shoulder. "Are you really coming and bringing that sign tomorrow?"

"Sure," he said. "I can do whatever I want. So *HA* on you!"

That evening, after Uncle Claude, Walt, and Jaroslav brought Grandma home again in the Elvis Mobile, we gathered in the den to watch TV and eat popcorn.

"Grandma? Did you know the town of Bentley was originally named *Bent Tree*?"

Everyone looked at me like I'd grown a third eye in the middle of my forehead. So I quickly explained what Jazz had read in her little blue paperback.

Grandma's eyes sparkled. "Why, I had no idea! Now those nincompoops in the city council will *have* to change their minds."

"Let's hope so," Mom said.

"Dudes!" Uncle Claude said. "You mean to say Groovy Granny didn't even know this town's named after that tree, yet she's been out there trying to protect it? Whoa, man. Granny rocks!"

Walt stood up and saluted Grandma.

So did Jaroslav. "Next to the King, Granny rulez!"

"Grandma? How could Bentley be named after a tree and no one even know it?"

Grandma hiked her shoulders. "I suppose through the years people just forgot."

I decided this would be a good time to tell everyone about the plan Jazz and I came up with at school today.

"And so," I concluded, "almost everyone in my class is going to join Grandma's protest." I looked around the room. "What do you think?"

"I think it's wonderful!" Dad said.

"Me, too, Chickadee!"

"Grandma?" I asked. "You know that vacant lot behind the grocery store? The one where the Dairy Hut used to be? Do you think the city council could put the pool there?"

Grandma shook her head. "I already checked. That lot doesn't meet city requirements. I checked on the two lots next to Dino's Reliable Used Cars, too, but Dino has already purchased them for future expansion of his business. There's bound to be somethin' available, even if it's not centrally located. It'll just take time to find it."

"Speaking of time," Dad said, pointing to his

watch. "Annie? If you're getting up early tomorrow morning, you better hit the sofa."

Grandma squeezed my hand. "Chickadee? I'll be more than proud to have your class out there with me tomorrow mornin'."

At 7:00 a.m., Grandma and I were the first ones to arrive at the large vacant lot where Elmer stood. Grandma poured a cup of coffee from her thermos and I poured hot chocolate from my own thermos, which Mom had insisted I bring along in my backpack. The air was cold and steam rose from our cups.

"So how many kids are comin'?" Grandma asked, taking a sip of her coffee.

"I'm not sure, but almost everyone raised their hand yesterday—even Leroy Kirk."

"That little rascal?"

We laughed and drank our coffee and hot chocolate, enjoying the crisp morning air.

"Okay, Chickadee. Chain me up!"

This time, I didn't hesitate. I grabbed the chain, the padlock, and *click!* My grandma was chained to Elmer.

After a couple hours of chanting and waving our signs, it was time for the others to show up.

One by one, my classmates started arriving. Some on in-line skates and skateboards. Others on bikes and in cars, all carrying their signs.

Jazz's dad dropped her off on his motorcycle. When she took off her helmet, her hair was all smushed and lopsided.

She grabbed my hands. "So what do you think, girlfriend? You like my newest glamour-girl hairstyle? It's all the rage in Hollywood, you know."

I didn't dare tell her that her hair looked like a football.

When the last few arrived by foot, we ended up with fourteen kids from my class, one tagalong little brother, three parents, and Dixie Lurken's black-and-white Border collie named Brutus. A pretty good turnout, I'd say.

"Okay, everybody!" I shouted. "Are we ready to save our town's history?"

"Yes!"

"I said, are we ready to save our town's history?"

"Yes!"

"Remember what Mrs. Hodge said," I warned. "No—"

"—Horsing around!" Mrs. Hodge finished.

I turned. "Mrs. Hodge! You're here!"

"Sure I am. I wouldn't let my class down." She gave everyone a hug, even Grandma. "Mrs. Glover? You're giving my students a hands-on experience they'll never forget. Thank you."

Grandma smiled proudly. "Just doin' my duty!"

"Class? Any questions before we begin our march?"

Leroy pushed through the crowd, hands on hips. "I don't have any questions, but I think you guys are making a big mistake. You're all going to end up in *tree jail*!"

"Leroy, there is no such thing as *tree jail*," Mrs. Hodge said. "Now let's march!"

"Save our native tree!"

"Don't!"

"Save our native tree!"

"Don't!"

Mrs. Hodge stopped marching and tapped Leroy on the head with her sign. "Leroy, why don't you go voice your opinion over there?" She pointed to the sidewalk.

Leroy stomped off like the big ol' baby that he was and stood there pouting, holding his DOWN WITH TREES sign.

In a matter of minutes a familiar white van pulled up: CHANNEL 8 NEWS—OUR NOSE KNOWS

NEWS. Out stepped Tony Zhang and his camera crew.

"Hey, fellas!" he shouted to his crew. "Get those cameras rolling! Pronto!"

My class marched back and forth, waving our signs, while Mrs. Hodge filled Tony in on what was happening.

"Save our native tree! Save our native tree!"

"This is Tony Zhang for Channel 8 News, where our nose knows news, reporting live from Sixth Street in downtown Bentley. The fourth-grade students from Mrs. Hodge's class at Will Rogers Elementary have joined forces with local activist Daisy Glover. They want to save Elmer, this massive American elm which is scheduled to be cut down Monday morning and replaced with a swimming-pool complex." He held his microphone up to Grandma. "What do you think about having schoolchildren join your efforts?"

"I couldn't be happier," Grandma said.

Tony held his microphone up to Mrs. Hodge. "What do you think about your students becoming activists?"

"I think it's great!" Mrs. Hodge said. Then she

put her hands on my shoulders. "This is Annie Glover, granddaughter of Daisy Glover."

"And what do *you* have to say, young lady?"

My knees knocked. "Um, I think it's important to let the city council know that the children of Bentley want to save this tree, too!"

Then Leroy walked over to the tree, waving his stupid ol' sign.

"And how about you, young man?" Tony asked. "I see you have a different opinion about trees."

"I'm allergic to trees. They make my eyes water and my nose itch and my throat clog and—"

"What he means to say," Jazz interrupted, stepping in front of Leroy, "is that even though he's tragically allergic to trees, he realizes the importance of *this* tree because our town is named after it."

Tony Zhang looked puzzled.

So did Leroy. "I didn't say that . . . *did I?*"

"You were *about* to say that," I insisted, walking him away from the camera.

With Leroy out of the way, Jazz covered her heart and explained what she'd discovered in

her little blue paperback about Bentley's original name. "So you see, this is the very-licious tree our town was named after!"

"Unbelievable!" the reporter said, then he looked directly into the camera. "Will the fourth-grade students from Will Rogers Elementary be able to change the city council's decision to cut down this 'very-licious' tree in less than forty-eight hours? This is Tony Zhang, and I'll be standing by, reporting live for Channel 8 News."

We continued marching, waving to the camera.

"Save our native tree!"

"Bent Tree! Bent-ley!"

Then the city manager pulled up.

"What's going on here?" Mr. Castillo demanded.

Nobody answered.

"Stop this! Stop this now!" he said, putting his hand over the camera. "You kids go home!"

But we didn't budge.

"Look, kids. You'll have to disperse!" he shouted.

Mrs. Hodge stepped forward. "My students and I are not leaving until you promise to protect this tree."

Mr. Castillo shook his head. "The city council has already made its decision. You and your students are trespassing. Now go home!"

But no one moved.

"We want to stay!"

"Yeah, we don't care if we're trespassing!"

"Elmer needs us!"

"Mr. Castillo? My students and I feel—"

"Take your students back home where they belong."

Mrs. Hodge looked at Mr. Castillo, then at us. "I'm sorry, class, but you heard the city manager. We better do as he says."

"No fair!"

"Yeah!"

"We were just getting started!"

Mrs. Hodge herded us across the street. When we got into our school's parking lot, dragging our signs and hopes behind us, she gave us a pep talk. "Class? At least we gave it a try. We did our best, and I'm proud of every one of you. Even you, Leroy."

"Me?" Leroy smiled and puffed out his chest. "Well, Jazz took the words right out of my mouth, you know."

We stood around for a few minutes watching

Mr. Castillo talk to Grandma. It looked like he'd given up and decided to let her stay. Then my classmates headed for home in all directions. Some phoned their parents and waited on the playground with Mrs. Hodge.

"Can I go to your house?" Jazz asked.

"Sure," I replied, but it just didn't feel right leaving Grandma.

As we got to the corner, I realized I'd forgotten my backpack and thermos. But when I turned around to go get it, Grandma was lying on the ground.

"Grandma! What happened?" I shouted, and we took off running toward her.

"Ooooh!" Grandma moaned. "I unlocked the chain so I could take a bathroom break at the gas station on the corner, and next thing I knew, I tripped over this backpack. I think I've sprained my ankle."

I felt horrible.

"Here, let us help you up, Grandma."

Jazz took one arm, I took the other, and we lifted her back to her feet.

"Ooooh. I don't think I can stand, Chickadee."

Poor Grandma. She winced in pain.

"I need to get off my foot."

"Lean on me," I said, putting my arm around her waist.

But Mr. Castillo motioned for us to leave. "You kids get going like the rest of your class. I'll make sure someone takes care of your grandmother, young lady. You there! Cameraman! Take this woman home so she can get off her feet!"

Jazz and I trudged back down the street, watching Grandma being led to the Channel 8 News van. With each wobbly step my poor ol' grandma took, I felt like a crumb bum, like a big, fat failure.

"Some good *we* did," I said.

"Yeah," Jazz agreed. "Our grand-erful plan turned out to be a grand-erful *flop*!"

An ULTRA-*MEGA*-LICIOUS PLAN

Grandma, are you okay? I'm so sorry. It's all my fault. I can't believe I forgot my backpack," I said when Jazz and I got home. We slumped down on the sofa, next to Grandma, and I lifted the ice bag off her ankle. It was black and blue and swollen.

Jazz covered her heart. "Oh, Mrs. G! Your ankle's totally tragic!"

"Girls, I'm proud of you. We made great progress out there today!"

Jazz and I looked at each other. "Progress?"

"Yes," Grandma said. "Thanks to you two and Channel 8 News, now everyone in Bentley will want to save Elmer."

But I wasn't so sure. "Yeah, and thanks to me, you're stuck on the sofa with an ice bag on your ankle."

Mom walked into the living room with the

newspaper and a cup of hot coffee for Grandma. "Daisy! Did you see the newspaper this morning? You made the front page!"

There on the front was a photo of Grandma chained to Elmer with a caption that read: "Local lady guards bent tree."

"More progress," Grandma said, smiling.

"Hey," Jazz said. "Let's show your uncle Claude."

Mom looked at her watch. "Oh my! Those three deadheads are still asleep. You two, go wake them up. They've got that big parachute jump for Dino's this afternoon. You know how long it takes them to primp in front of the mirror. They're worse than teenage girls on prom night."

Jazz and I walked down the hallway and knocked on my bedroom door.

"Pssst! Uncle Claude? Grandma made the front page!"

We heard a *thunk* and some shuffles.

"I think you woke him up," Jazz whispered.

In a few seconds, the door opened, and there stood Uncle Claude, yawning.

"Dudettes! Don't you realize me and my boys need twelve full hours of beauty sleep if we're going to look like the King?"

We didn't know that. "But Grandma's in the newspaper," I said, "and Mom said you need to get ready for your parachute jump today."

He rubbed his eyes and looked at his watch. "Whoa! Aces from outer spaces! Wake up! We've only got four hours to turn ourselves into Elvis!" He slammed the door in our faces, then opened it up an inch and took the newspaper. "Thank you. Thank you very much!"

That afternoon, Grandma's ankle grew to the size of a baseball, so Dad dropped Jazz off at her house and we took Grandma to the emergency room. After three hours of waiting and two bags of stale pretzels from the vending machine, I was happy to see her being wheeled back into the waiting room. The doctor said there were no broken bones, just a sprain, and he gave her a prescription for pain pills and recommended crutches.

We got home just in time to prop Grandma up on the sofa and turn on the six o'clock Channel 8 News. I felt a little nervous waiting for my class's segment. I'd never been on TV before.

"Hey! There it is!" My heart did a little flip-flop. "There we are!"

The camera zoomed in on Grandma's interview, then my interview, then my class marching and chanting, waving into the camera.

"Annie, you look so grown up," Mom said. "And so does Jazz, but what's that on her head?"

"Looks like a football," Dad said.

I laughed. "It's one of her new glamour-girl hairstyles."

After a few commercials, the news came back on, and this time a woman reporter was standing in a crowd of people with balloons and streamers. Above her head towered a huge, green blow-up dinosaur.

"Look!" Mom said. "Here comes Claude's jump from this afternoon. Everybody be quiet."

Dad raised his eyebrows. "Speaking of Claude, shouldn't those three be home by now?"

Mom shook her head. "They called me on my cell while you were helping Grandma get into the car. Said they met some 'awesome chicks' who were Elvis fans and they were going to take them cruising in the Elvis Mobile."

"Well, all I've got to say is they better not come home at two in the morning!" Dad said.

"Shh," Mom insisted, pointing to the TV.

"This is Deborah Leigh Gooding. I'm here at

Dino's Reliable Used Cars for a special celebration. Dino? Tell us about it."

"We're celebrating thirty years of reliable used car sales," Dino said, wearing huge green glasses shaped like a dinosaur. "We've got all our cars marked down thirty percent. Free hot dogs! Free dinosaur coloring books! And we've even got the Flying Elvis Trio!"

The camera rolled upward and captured Uncle Claude, Walt, and Jaroslav parachuting from an airplane in full Elvis attire. They did a few flips and spins, then spiraled downward, landing on the large vacant lots next to Dino's, which had been roped off from the crowd.

"Would you look at all those people!" Grandma said. "Must be nearly a hundred!"

"More like *two* hundred," Dad said, looking amazed.

"I had no idea my little brother could draw such a huge crowd!"

Neither did I, and seeing that crowd gave me an idea. An idea so wonderful, I had to run to my bedroom, lock the door, and do some serious thinking.

Stepping over a pillow, two empty pizza boxes

that smelled like onions, and a duffel bag that smelled even worse, I held my nose and sat down at my desk.

It was covered with the three Kings of Rock-and-Roll's junk—beauty cream, a box of Elvis chest hair, foot fungus spray, and heartburn medicine. I moved it out of the way, clearing off a place for me to think, and grabbed a piece of paper from my drawer.

I searched through the coffee can that held all my pens and pencils, looking for my newest purchase—the pen with ten different colors of ink that I had bought at the book fair.

I tried out all the colors, then clicked it to orange and jotted down my idea. *Click!* Another idea in blue. *Click!* Another in purple. Before I knew it and before the Elvises got back to kick me out of my own room again, I had a whole rainbow of ideas turned into my best plan yet. A plan so ultra-licious that even Jazz herself would be impressed.

Later that night, when the Elvises came home totally hyped up and hungry as horses, we all sat down at the dining room table, talking about their jump. DD hung out under the table, sniffing shoes and looking for handouts.

"I sure was proud of you," Mom said, patting Uncle Claude's arm. She set out a late-night snack of pimento cheese sandwiches cut into little squares, and everyone dove in.

"I couldn't believe the crowd," I told them.

"Me, neither," Dad said.

"Dudes! It was awesome!" Uncle Claude said. "The crowd, the cameras, the awesome chicks!"

"True," Jaroslav said. "Awesome cheeks love riding in the Elviz Mobile!"

While everyone—even Dad, who had made a special trip to the grocery store for two more cartons of Nutty Buddy Chocolate Swirl—was laughing and in a good mood, I snuck a corner of my sandwich under the table for DD and then shared my ultra-licious plan to save Elmer.

"So will you help?" I asked, looking around the table.

"You bet!"

"Sure we will!"

"I'll help as much as this foot will let me," Grandma said.

"Can DD come, too? *Pleeaase?*" I begged.

Mom looked at Dad. "I don't see why not."

Uncle Claude gave me a high five. "Annie Girl, me and my dudes with attitudes would be honored to help out."

Before I went to bed, or should I say *sofa*, I phoned Jazz.

"Hello?"

"Hello, Jazz? I've got an *ultra-licious* plan to save Elmer."

"Wait a minute," she said. "That's *my* word."

"I know, but can I borrow it?"

The line was silent. "Well . . . it depends. What's your plan?"

"Monday morning before school I'm going to chain myself to Elmer."

I heard a gasp. "Did you just say you're going to—"

"Yeah. And I need you to do it with me."

Another gasp.

"We took Grandma to the emergency room this afternoon. She's okay, but she has to stay off her feet. Doctor's orders. So Elmer needs us now more than ever!"

"But what about Mr. Castillo?" Jazz asked.

"He might throw us in jail. And what about school? We might get suspended or something."

"Jazz, it's a chance we'll have to take."

"Oh, Annie-Ba-Nannie!" she squealed. "I *love* it! It'll be deliciously romantic."

"I knew you'd say that."

"Just think," Jazz said. "One day . . . years from now . . . our very own children will be climbing Elmer . . . and reading books in Elmer . . . all because of us!"

"I hope so," I said. "Is it a deal? Will you chain yourself to Elmer with me?"

"Absolutely. But let me ask my dad," she said, and I could hear her putting down the phone. "Da-ad!"

In a minute or two, she picked the phone back up. "Okay, girlfriend, it's a real deal."

"And no matter what anyone says, even Mr. Castillo, you'll do it?"

"In a heartbeat!"

"Guess who's going to help us?"

"Who?"

"My whole family—Mom, Dad, Grandma. Even DD. But Dad says Grandma has to stay off her feet. And guess who *else*?"

"Who?"

"My uncle Claude and his Elvis buddies."

"Hey, I saw them on TV tonight. They're hilarious."

"So you'll meet me at the tree Monday before school?"

"You bet, and I'll bring my sign," Jazz said.

"So is it okay if I call my plan *ultra-licious*?" I asked.

"Annie-Ba-Nannie, this plan of yours is not only ultra-licious, it's ultra-*mega*-licious!"

Early Monday morning, I put DD on his leash and tied a red bandanna around his neck for good luck. Together, we bravely walked to the vacant lot carrying Grandma's chain in my backpack.

When we got there, I hooked DD's leash onto one of Elmer's branches. "There you go, DD. You want Elmer saved, too. Don't you, boy?"

I searched Elmer's trunk with its many carvings. I saw "Be MINE 4 ever." I saw lots and lots of initials. Then I found the ones I was looking for—"R.G. + C.K."—my dad's and mom's with a heart drawn around them.

Standing on tiptoe, I traced the heart with my finger.

"This is it, DD. I'm really going to do this."

He looked up at me with his cute brown eyes, wagging his scruffy tail. Then he hiked his leg on the tree trunk, which I think was his stamp of approval.

Swallowing the giant lump in my throat, I wrapped Grandma's chain around me and Elmer. I opened the padlock and *click!*

There I stood—in Grandma's place—chained to Elmer. An ocean of thoughts flooded my head. *I'm crazy for doing this. No, I'm not. I can't do this. Yes, I can.*

Cars sped by as I waved my sign.

"Save our native tree!" I shouted. *"Save our native tree!"*

A teenage boy leaned his head out the window of a passing car. "Hey, punk! You and your dog go home! I want that pool!"

An oil truck rattled by, and DD ran to the end of his leash, barking.

"That's it, DD. Tell them you want this tree, too!"

Twelve cars. A limousine. Seven trucks.

My head was still flooded with thoughts.

Why didn't I just stay home? No, this is where I need to be. Can I really do this? Yes, I know I can.

"Save our native tree! Save our native tree!"

Four more cars. A bus. And a tow truck.

Is Jazz ever going to get here? What if she's changed her mind and I'm stuck out here all by myself? Can I do this on my own?

Finally, Jazz came running across the street with another one of her glamour-girl hairstyles. This one looked pretty good. At least, it didn't look like a football.

"How's it going?"

"Great," I said, thrilled to see her. But inside I was a nervous wreck.

Jazz gave DD a good belly rub, then pulled her sign from her backpack and grabbed my hand. "Annie-Ba-Nannie? You are no longer a lone girl . . . chained to a tree . . . you now have me to stand with you as sister tree lovers . . . upholding justice and fighting for liber-tree."

I cracked up laughing. "Liber-tree? That's a good one. We should put that on a sign."

"Yeah," Jazz agreed. *"Give me liber-tree or give me death!"*

Getting out my key, I unlocked the padlock.

"Are you ready?" I asked.

"Ready!"

She stepped inside the chain with me and—*click!*—we were both chained to Elmer.

Jazz grabbed my hands and looked at me real serious. "Isn't this the most deliciously romantic thing you've ever done in your whole entire life?"

Delicious and *romantic* weren't exactly the words I would have chosen. More like *brave, scary,* or even *crazy.*

"I can't wait to grow up and tell my children about this someday," Jazz said. "They'll think we're modern-day, ultra-licious heroes, you know. Just like Lady Godiva."

"Ja-azz. Before you start comparing us to Lady Godiva, shouldn't we save Elmer first?"

"Yeah, you're right," she said and held up her sign. "Let's go for it!"

"Save our native tree! Save our native tree!"

"Bent Tree! Bent-ley! Save our native tree!"

As more buses and cars pulled into our school's parking lot, our classmates raced over to see what we were doing.

"This is awesome!" Dave Goldberg said, flashing his magazine smile. "Are you two *really* chained to Elmer?"

Jazz and I smiled and showed him the padlock.

"Yo-ho-ho and a bottle of rum!" Martin shouted, running across the street. He was wearing his eye patch and had a bandanna wrapped over his head. "What *ARRRRR* you doin' over here?"

"Protecting Elmer," I said.

Martin bent down and scratched DD's ears. "Whose dog?"

"Mine," I said. "His name is DD, short for Dirty Dog."

"Dirty Dog? I once knew a pirate named Dirty Dog. He never took a bath. Smelled like a fish all the time. I made him walk the plank 'cause he was drawin' flies."

I looked at Jazz and we cracked up laughing. *How does he come up with this ridiculous stuff?*

Dixie Lurken pedaled by on her bicycle, then backed up to take another look. "Oh my gosh! What are you guys doing?"

"We're lone girls . . . fighting for justice," Jazz replied.

"I'm a lone girl. Can I fight for justice, too?" Dixie asked.

"What about me?" Martin asked. "I'm a lone pirate. Pirates like to fight. We'll fight for *anything*!"

Before I knew it, my whole entire class, minus

Leroy, had meandered over to join us. Some of their parents and their little brothers and sisters joined us, too. Even Dixie's dog, Brutus, showed up with her parents, which was fine by DD because then he had a buddy.

Mom and Dad arrived with Grandma. After unloading two chairs from the trunk of our car, Dad helped Grandma get settled. She sat in one and propped her foot on the other.

Mrs. Hodge must have noticed all the commotion, because she came walking across the street with a heaping tray of her famous chocolate-chip cookies. "Good morning!" she said to everyone, offering us cookies. They were still nice and warm. "Care if I join your protest—at least until the first bell rings?"

Good ol' Mrs. Hodge.

When the Channel 8 News crew arrived, setting up their cameras and equipment, I felt so proud I thought I'd bust a button off my coat.

"This is Tony Zhang, reporting live from Sixth Street in downtown Bentley. As you can see, there is an overwhelming response by the fourth-grade students from Will Rogers Elementary to save Elmer the American elm. In fact, two students have chained themselves to this tree which is in danger of being cut down any minute." He looked at his watch. "Or should I say, any second!"

Bus 40 pulled up into the school parking lot, and I bit my lip, wondering if Leroy was on it. Sure enough, he ran across the street and with a mad face he shouted, "My dad's on his way right now! His chain saw is really sharp! So *HA* on all of you!"

DON'T BE CRUEL

"*SAVE OUR NATIVE TREE! BENT TREE! BENT-LEY!*"

I looked at my watch: 8:07. Uncle Claude should have been here by now. Then I panicked, remembering how those three liked to sleep late. *Oh no! What if they're still in bed getting their twelve hours of Elvis beauty sleep? What if they can't get ahold of the guy who flies the airplane?*

A car pulled up, and out stepped Mr. Castillo. "Who's the leader of this group?"

I looked over at Grandma, sitting there with her sprained ankle. She nodded at me. So I gulped and raised my hand. "I . . . I am, sir."

"You again. I appreciate your concern for this tree, young lady, but I don't want to have to call the sheriff out here. You girls unchain yourselves now and go to school. The rest of you go about your business."

I jutted out my chin the same way I'd seen Grandma do. "I'm not leaving," I said. "And neither is Jazz."

"Yeah," Jazz agreed. "This tree is too fabtastical to cut down for a parking lot. It has a right to live!"

The crowd cheered.

I looked up at the sky, and then at my watch, again: 8:12. *Where's Uncle Claude? He was supposed to be here twelve minutes ago.*

"*ELMER! ELMER! ELMER!*" the crowd chanted.

Mr. Castillo looked a little stunned. He pulled out his cell phone and began dialing. "Girls, you've left me no alternative. I'm calling the sheriff."

The first bell rang. Mrs. Hodge gathered our classmates together and began to lead them toward the school. Then I heard it—faint at first, but definitely the sound of an airplane.

"Look!" I shouted, pointing to the sky. "Look! They're here! The Flying Elvis Trio!"

The crowd looked up, watching the plane

glide in closer and closer. Its door opened. "Jail-house Rock" blared from speakers inside. Streamers and confetti filled the air as the plane circled round and round and the crowd grew larger.

Cars pulled over to the side of the road.

People ran out of their houses.

Mrs. Hodge and my class stopped in their tracks in the school parking lot. Practically every kid and teacher in Will Rogers Elementary ran out to join them.

"SAVE OUR NATIVE TREE! BENT TREE! BENT-LEY!"

Then black and pink balloons dropped from the plane and the Flying Elvis Trio jumped out, flipping and twirling and falling at rapid speed. Down, down they came, toward a large section of the vacant lot which Mom and Dad had roped off first thing this morning.

"Elvis! Elvis!" screamed the crowd.

As their parachutes dragged across the ground and they came to a running stop, all three of them unbuckled their helmets and started singing, "Don't be cruel to a tree that's true. Don't be cruel, this tree belongs to you. Don't want no other tree-eee. Baby, it's this tree I'm dreaming of!"

The crowd pressed in closer.

"Elvis? Can I have your autograph?"

"Elvis! Elvis!"

"I love you, Elvis! All *three* of you!"

"Thank you. Thank you very much," Uncle Claude said, doing a few karate kicks. Obviously, he, Walt, and Jaroslav knew how to work a crowd. They mingled about, hugging all the ladies and posing for pictures with their lips curled.

Then a lime green pickup stopped in the street.

Holding a chain saw, Leroy's dad made his way through the crowd and stood beside Mr. Castillo. They talked in low voices.

Grandma limped over on her crutches and looked them both in the eye. "Gentlemen, this tree belongs to all of us—you, me, these children, and these parents. We're *not* lettin' you cut Elmer down."

Mr. Kirk pulled the cord on his chain saw.

REM-rem-rem-rem-rem-rem-rmmmm!

"See? I told you his chain saw was really sharp!" Leroy shouted. "You better get out of the way or he'll cut you right in half!"

Jazz gasped and looked real serious. "Oh my gosh! This isn't just deliciously romantic, it's *totally tragic*! Annie-Ba-Nannie? Sister tree lover? Are you prepared to be sawed in half for the good of our community?"

"Ja–azz. We're not going to be sawed in half for the good of our community, so get that out of your head."

Tony Zhang held up his microphone to Mr. Castillo. "The chain saw is running. The people of Bentley want this tree saved. Now what are you going to do?"

"Well . . . you see," Mr. Castillo stammered. "The swimming-pool complex will need more—"

Rem-rem-rem-REM-rem-remmmmm!

"SAVE OUR NATIVE TREE! BENT TREE! BENT-LEY!"

"This tree is taking up parking spaces, and what I'm trying to say is—"

I tugged on Mr. Castillo's coat sleeve. "Mr. Castillo? We hear what you're trying to say. But what *we* are trying to say is this tree is our history—and this is *my* history." I stood on tiptoe, pointing to my parents' initials.

"The fact is, oh, forget it!" He threw his hands into the air, shaking his head. "The truth is, I want this tree, too. Mr. Kirk? The city won't need your services after all." Then to the rest of us he shouted, "I'm calling an emergency city council meeting this evening to decide where we can put the swimming-pool complex! If any of you have any suggestions, I hope you'll attend the meeting. How about seven o'clock? In the city hall."

Tony Zhang smiled into the camera. "As you can see, the town of Bentley has saved their namesake, and plans are already under way for the swimming-pool complex to be built at a new location. If you have any suggestions for this location, contact the city council or attend their emergency council meeting tonight in *Bent Tree* City Hall. This is Channel 8 News, where our nose knows news, and *this* is good news!"

Everyone went bananas, hugging Grandma, hugging me, hugging DD, hugging people they didn't even know. The three Elvises were hugged so much by all the ladies, they had permanent smiles on their faces.

"We did it! We did it!" I told Grandma. "We saved Elmer!"

"We sure did, Chickadee."

"Annie-Ba-Nannie! Isn't it fab? Like totally glorious?" Jazz said, covering her heart. "I can see it now . . . you, me, and Mrs. G . . . our photo on

the front page of the newspaper . . . signing autographs . . . being interviewed on TV . . . maybe even meeting the president of the United States himself!"

"Ja–azz!"

Back in Room 4B, everyone buzzed about, glowing from our accomplishment and all talking at once.

"We did it!"

"We saved our town's namesake!"

"Now we're getting Elmer *and* a pool!"

"Yeah. And it all started with Annie-Fannie-Wannie's crazy ol' grandma."

Leroy was trying to get under my skin again, but there was no way I was going to let it happen. Not on a glorious day like this one.

Unzipping his emergency medical kit, he pulled out his magnifying glass and looked at me, one eye bigger than the other.

"See my new shoes?" He lifted up his foot. "I begged Grandpa Joe to buy them at the mall yesterday. They've got electromagnetic fibers built into the soles. Now I can run faster than anybody in this room. So *HA* on you, you tree lover!"

"Leroy, shoes can't make you run faster. The only way anyone can run faster is just by practicing. But you are right about one thing."

"What?"

I got right in his face. "Annie-Glover's-a-tree-lover-Annie-Glover's-a-tree-lover!"